Praise for

Lulu

and the Duck in the Park

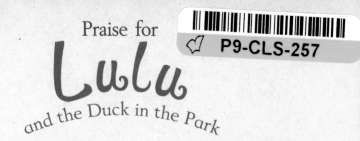

★ "McKay shows a rare ability to capture a younger audience in this involving chapter book for transitional readers. The well-structured, third-person narrative builds dramatic tension, provides comic relief of the most believable sort, and shows plenty of heart."—*Booklist* starred review

★ "A warmhearted beginning to a new chapter book series delights from the first few sentences…What Lulu and Mellie do to protect the egg, get through class, and not outrage Mrs. Holiday is told so simply and rhythmically and so true to the girls' perfectly-logical-for-third-graders' thinking, that it will beguile young readers completely."—*Kirkus Reviews* starred review

★ "McKay's pacing is spot-on, and the story moves briskly. Lamont's black-and-white illustrations capture the sparkle in Lulu's eyes and the warmth and fuzziness of a newly hatched duckling. The satisfying ending will have children awaiting the next installment in what is likely to become a hit series for fans of other plucky characters like Horrible Harry, Stink, and Junie B. Jones."—*School Library Journal* starred review

★ "'Lulu was famous for animals,' opens this sparkling series launch…Though aimed at a younger audience than McKay's Exiles novels and series about the Casson family, this offering has similarly abundant humor and heart."—*Publishers Weekly* starred review

★ "McKay introduces complex characters, and animal-loving Lulu's dilemma rings true."—*Horn Book* starred review

"Lulu, whose personality reminds me a lot of Ramona Quimby and Clementine, is the kind of good-hearted, bold character kids really relate to and root for."—*Secrets & Sharing Soda*

"This is what an early chapter book should be!!"—*LiterariTea*

A Junior Library Guild selection

Lulu
and the Dog from the Sea

Hilary McKay

Illustrated by Priscilla Lamont

Albert Whitman & Company
Chicago, Illinois

For Lissy, with love from
Nanny Kath and Hilary McKay

Library of Congress Cataloging-in-Publication Data

McKay, Hilary.
Lulu and the dog from the sea / by Hilary McKay ;
illustrated by Priscilla Lamont.
p. cm.
Summary: Seven-year-old Lulu and her cousin think
their vacation house is the most perfect place ever until
they find a trouble-prone stray dog living on the beach.
[1. Dogs—Fiction. 2. Beaches—Fiction. 3. Vacations—Fiction.]
I. Lamont, Priscilla, ill. II. Title.
PZ7.M4786574Ld 2013
[Fic]—dc23
2012013697

Text copyright © 2011 by Hilary McKay
Illustrations copyright © 2011 by Priscilla Lamont
First published in the UK by Scholastic Children's Books,
an imprint of Scholastic Ltd.
Hardcover edition first published in the United States of America
in 2013 by Albert Whitman & Company
Paperback edition first published in the United States of America
in 2014 by Albert Whitman & Company
ISBN 978-0-8075-4821-9 (paperback)
ISBN 978-0-8075-4822-6 (ebook)

Printed in the United States of America
14 13 12 11 10 9 LB 24 23 22 21 20 19

For more information about Albert Whitman & Company,
visit our website at www.albertwhitman.com.

Chapter One

The Cottage by the Sea

Lulu and Mellie were seven years old. They
were cousins and they
were friends. Their
houses were so close
that it took less than
five minutes to run
between the two. They
could visit each other
easily without getting
lost or squished on
the road.

That was a good thing, because Lulu and Mellie were not just ordinary friends—they were best friends.

They were such good friends they hardly ever fought, although sometimes they did grumble at each other a little. They mostly grumbled about each other's hobbies, which were not at all alike.

"Coloring again?" Lulu would say when she went to see why Mellie had forgotten to come and play. "You're *always* coloring!"

"Cleaning again?" Mellie would ask when she came to find out what Lulu had been doing all day. "You're *always* cleaning!" she would say, holding her nose.

It wasn't true that Mellie was always coloring. Often she was painting or drawing or making things with glue and glitter and chopped-up paper and causing a mess. But it was true that very often Lulu was cleaning.

Lulu loved animals and she had a lot of pets.

The rule about pets in Lulu's house was: *The more the merrier! As long as Lulu cleans up after them!*

Lulu had two guinea pigs, four rabbits, one parrot, one hamster, a lot of goldfish, and a rather old dog named Sam.

It took a lot of work to look after all these pets. Mostly Lulu did it, but sometimes other people helped her out.

Whenever Lulu's family went on vacation, Mellie's parents would always help. They would do a swap—Lulu's family would take Mellie on vacation, and Mellie's family would take care of Lulu's pets.

All except for Sam the dog, who was going on vacation too. They were all going to stay in a cottage by the sea.

Sam did not think much of that. He didn't enjoy the seaside. He wasn't fond of sand, he didn't like chilly breezes, and he hated getting wet in cold, salty water. Sam was a small, golden, teddy-bear-shaped dog. He had short teddy bear legs, and a round teddy bear tummy, and a sweet, stubborn, sleepy teddy bear face.

When Sam went on vacation he took a lot

of luggage, all packed for him by Lulu. He took his red blanket and his water bowl and his food dish and his special dog biscuits. Also his dog leash and his dog towels in case he got wet, and his shampoo and his brushes in case he got sticky.

Sam also took his basket and his red velvety beanbag.

Sam loved his beanbag very much and if

he did not have it in his basket he could not go to sleep. Nobody else could go to sleep either, because Sam walked around howling and whining and moaning. It was very important not to forget the beanbag. Lulu's father checked a dozen times that it was safely in the car. He did not want to have to drive all the way home for it in the middle of the night, as he had once had to do.

Sam's luggage took up so much space that it was a good thing Lulu and Mellie had brought as little as possible. Their only big thing was Mellie's build-your-own-kite-kit. Mellie had been given this for a birthday present. She had opened it to admire the strings and the special kite paper, the bright pens, and the exciting instructions. But then she had put it away again to save for this seaside vacation.

Now the kite kit was on the backseat. All the things that would not fit any-where else were there too, piled around Lulu and Mellie.

"It's part of the vacation feeling," said Mellie. "Being all squished up, hardly able to breathe."

"It's fair that Sam should have the most space," agreed Lulu, "because really he'd rather not come on vacation at all. He'd rather be comfortable."

"This might be a comfortable vacation!" said Lulu's mother hopefully. That made everyone hoot with laughter. They spent the first part of the journey reminding one another about vacations in the past.

"Like the time we went camping and left behind the bag that had everyone's shoes," said Lulu.

 7

"Or that house we stayed in that had a ghost in the attic," said Mellie.

"Or that place where the chimney was struck by lightning and fell down into the living room," said Lulu's father.

Lulu's mother groaned and said perhaps they should turn back and not go away after all.

"They were nice vacations," said Lulu and Mellie, who had enjoyed the lightning and the ghost and the new shoes very much.

They were really looking forward to staying in a little seaside town.

That was what they thought, but the first thing they discovered about the cottage was that it was not near the town at all. It was all on its own, down a bumpy, potholed road. Bumps made Sam sick. So Lulu's father drove very slowly, trying to dodge the biggest holes, while Lulu's mother twisted around, watching for the gulps that meant Sam had to be flung out of the car as quickly as possible. Meanwhile, Mellie was ignoring both Sam and the bumpy road and saying, "Should I unpack my kite now, now that we're almost there? I think I could just open it and get out the parts…"

"No!" said Lulu's mother and father, but they said it too late. Mellie was already unpacking the kit. When the car fell into another hole, important-looking pieces of kite spilled everywhere, and Mellie began to moan.

"Just what I didn't want to happen!" she grumbled, turning herself upside down to try and gather the pieces from the floor.

"They call this a road?" complained Lulu's father. "It's just one giant crater after another!"

"Now the string's unwound!" cried Mellie.

Sam made a noise like a sort of cough.

"Almost there, Sam!" said Lulu's mother hopefully, rolling down her window.

Only Lulu sat quietly, gazing at the view. Ahead, she saw a white cottage and green grass. Every few minutes, she saw glimpses of a sea that gleamed dark gray or silver bright.

All along the edge of the sea Lulu could see a mountain range of sand dunes. Strange bushes grew on them with

dim gray leaves and orange berries.
Strange ribbonlike blue-green grasses were
combed by the sea wind. Strange narrow
sandy paths twisted and climbed and
suddenly vanished.

And all among the bushes and grass and
sandy paths a strange animal leaped and ran,
watching the car. It moved so quickly that
the only thing Lulu could see clearly was
its strange, flapping ears.

They were ears like brown paper bags.

The owner of the cottage was waiting for them when they arrived. Everyone except Mellie (who was still picking up pieces of kite) tumbled out of the car, all stiff and achy from traveling.

"Took your time, didn't you?" said the cottage owner as Lulu's parents smiled and called hello. "I saw you, dithering along that road, like there was all the time in the world!"

"Well!" began Lulu's father. "It's quite an obstacle course, that road…"

"You've got the wrong kind of car!" said the cottage owner. "You need something much bigger! Hurry up! Come inside and I'll give you the key. Shoes off!" she added sternly.

"It's very kind of you to wait," said Lulu's

mother, as she and Lulu's
father followed her to
the door.

"Had to," snapped the
cottage owner grimly.
"I needed to warn you
about that dog!"

"Sam?" asked Lulu, but
the cottage owner had
disappeared, with Lulu's
parents after her.

Bang! went the door in
a most unfriendly way.

"Why's she so…"
began Mellie, staring.

"Shush!" warned Lulu.

"…angry?" finished Mellie loudly, dropping
pieces of kite all over the ground as she spoke.
"Don't worry! She can't hear! She shut the door.
Why do you think she said that about Sam?"

Lulu couldn't imagine. Sam was behaving perfectly. He had survived the bumps without getting sick, and now he was doing what he always did at the end of a car journey: unpacking his food bowl.

On days when Sam was going for a ride in the car he was only ever given a very small breakfast. Now he wanted the rest of it. He stood up on his teddy bear legs, dragged his bowl out from his mountain of luggage, carried it in his teeth to Lulu, and dropped it at her feet.

It was Lulu's job to fill it up as quickly as possible.

As usual, she rushed to do it, and as usual Sam stood and watched, stumpy tail wagging, with a smile on his teddy bear face.

From inside the cottage Lulu's parents could see all this happening. Lulu's mother asked worriedly, "Why do you want to warn us about our dog? We did tell you we were bringing him."

"Your dog?" asked the cottage owner, looking out of the window at the happy sight of Sam gobbling dog food. "I wasn't talking about your dog! He's a poor old thing, isn't he? Looks more like a sheep… *That* dog!"

She jabbed a pointing finger in the direction of the sand dunes, where a small sandstorm had just erupted.

The sandstorm rolled down the sand dunes, arrived between Lulu and Mellie in a cloud of dust, seized the packet of dog food that Lulu had only a moment before put down, whirled around, and raced away, all in one astonishing moment.

"*RUFF! RUFF! RUFF!*" barked Sam, nearly falling over with rage.

 15

"*That* dog!" said the cottage owner, rushing out of the cottage with Lulu's parents behind her. "That dog!" she repeated, pointing to a dusty blur on the sand dunes. "That dog from the sea! He's a thief! He's a menace! The people last week lost a whole roasted chicken from under their noses! Nothing is safe from him and no one can get near him. We've had the dogcatcher out twice already and he's never gotten close enough to grab—"

"Oh, poor dog!" exclaimed Lulu.

"Don't you go encouraging him," said the woman, turning on Lulu quite fiercely. "He's not welcome around here! You'll have to be careful. No leaving out picnics or scraps for the seagulls. He goes through all the trash too. So you'll have to remember to take the trash can into the house at night!"

"*Take the trash can into the house at night?*" repeated Lulu's father, staring.

"I've warned you and now I need to go," said the cottage owner.

"Did you say, 'Take…'?"

"I did," said the cottage owner, dragging a bike from the hedge. Then she handed Lulu's mother a large and rather rusty key and rode off.

"*Take the trash can into the house at night!*" exploded Lulu's father wildly the moment she was gone. "What kind of place is it where you have to do that?"

Lulu and Mellie became helpless with giggles and rolled around on the grass.

"And you're not helping!" complained Lulu's father as he stepped over them.

"Oh!" said Mellie. "I love this place!"

"You haven't seen the inside yet," warned Lulu's mother. "And neither have we, hardly! I thought she might stay and show us where things are…and explain about hot water and how the stove works…Oh well, never mind! Who's coming with me to explore?"

Lulu and Mellie scrambled to their feet and hurried to follow her into the cottage.

It was very clean.

And very bare.

It was just four little rooms: two bedrooms, a kitchen, and a living room, with a very damp-smelling bathroom tacked onto the back. The water in the faucet was as cold as ice, and the oven (said a neat label that was stuck on the front) was missing a part.

"No wonder Mrs.-on-the-Bike ran away so fast!" said Lulu's father, and he went outside and looked suspiciously at the chimney to see if it had been struck by lightning. It looked solid, however, and there was no ghost in the attic because there was no attic. There was no upstairs at all.

"Well, at least we all have shoes this time!" said Lulu's father, cheering up. "So maybe we'll survive!"

Lulu and Mellie were sure they would. Their bedroom window faced the sand dunes. They pushed it open and the sea wind blew in, and there they were, nearly among the blue-green grasses and gray, orange-berried bushes. Almost next to the little gold paths down which a dog from the sea might swoop like a storm.

"It's the most perfect place ever," said Lulu.

Her mother said "Hmmm" to that. She was exploring the kitchen cupboards. She had just discovered that there were not enough mugs for all four of them to have hot drinks at once, and not enough glasses for all four of them to have cold drinks at once either. And she discovered other things about saucepans and forks and spoons that made her say "Hmmm" as well.

"But we *do* have shoes," said Lulu's father. "So let's go and explore!"

So they did.

Chapter Two

The Dog from the Sea

"I would like to know much, much more about the dog from the sea," said Lulu.

There was no sign of him in the sand dunes, nor on the wide windy beach. No dog with paper-bag ears splashed in the pools by the breakwaters, or raced across the golf course (where no dogs were allowed). But as they got nearer to the town end of the beach they heard news.

The ice cream and hot dog stand knew

him very well. They had lost more than one sausage to his thieving ways.

The lady from the bucket and shovel shop said, "Shocking!"

What else could you say about a dog who helped himself to the most expensive sort of wood-handled shovel? Who lifted it from its box by the postcard stand, galloped off with it clamped in his jaws, chewed it to shreds, left the bits on the sand, and came back, tail wagging, for another!

"But where did he come from?" asked Lulu.

"He came from the back of the Golden Lotus," said the lady from the bucket and shovel shop.

The Golden Lotus was a Chinese restaurant. There was a whole street of little restaurants in the town. Indian and Chinese and Italian and Thai and a fish and chip shop at the end. And behind the shops was a small messy space, full of crates and boxes, trash cans, recycling bins, and other things like old fridges waiting to be taken away.

It was a big untidy muddle, the shop lady told Lulu, and in the most untidy bit of the muddle, under a pile of crates and cardboard boxes behind the Golden Lotus, the mother of the dog from the sea had made a den.

 25

Three puppies had been born in that den: the dog from the sea and the dog from the sea's two sisters.

All through the spring they lived together, a wild and happy life. In the daytime they slept, all flung in a warm heap under the crates.

At night they went hunting with their mother. She was a very clever dog, and she knew all the places to find things to eat. Seaside towns with hungry visitors have lots of spare food, either thrown into trash cans or dropped on the streets. The mother dog taught her three puppies how to crawl under the fence near the fairground to get to the large garbage bins. She showed them how to push over a trash can, and how to chase a seagull from a handful of chips. She showed her wild family every single thing it was possible for a dog to eat.

What good dogs, thought Lulu as she listened. What a lot of cleaning up they had done. People should have been very grateful, she thought.

But people were not grateful. Not even at the Golden Lotus, where the dogs cleared up most of all.

They sent for the dogcatcher.

Two dogcatchers came. A very tall man and a very tall woman. They spoke to the dogs with kind voices.

First they caught the two sisters. They put them in two cages, where they howled and cried so loudly their mother came to rescue them.

That made it easy for the dogcatchers to catch her as well.

Very soon there were three dogs in three cages.

The last of the wild dog family watched in horror. He did not know what happened to a dog after it was caught in a cage. He had never heard of vets or rescue homes or the friendly people who visit them and say, "*That's the dog for me!*" All he knew was what he saw and heard: his sisters crying, his mother frantic, tearing at the cage.

He watched, but he watched from a distance. He guessed they had a cage for him too, and he was right—they did.

But they could not get him into it.

When the dogcatchers turned to the last wild dog, and spoke in their kind voices, the wild dog ran for his life.

He ran to the sand dunes, and there he hid.

That was how the wild dog became the dog from the sea.

For a long time he would sneak back to the crate pile behind the Golden Lotus, just in case the dogcatchers had changed their minds and allowed his family to come back. But at last he gave up hope.

He lived among the sand dunes, a wild hungry life. He stole all he could, and he ate whatever he could swallow, and sometimes it made him ill and sometimes it made him stronger. He got used to that. He got used to the long thirsty waits to drink from the stream that crossed the golf course or from the kiddie pool near the town. He got used to cold winds and the thorns on the gray bushes, but he never got used to being alone.

The dog from the sea was terribly lonely.

As the weather grew warmer, more and more people came to the beach. Grown-up people and children. The dog from the sea kept away from the grown-ups in case they had cages, but he watched the children. He was tremendously interested in the games they played and the holes they dug and the balls they threw. He watched from the sand dunes, wagging his tail, bouncing with excitement when they yelled at the waves, drooling as they ate their picnics.

When the beach emptied at night-time he inspected the places where they had been. Sometimes he found a lost toy. These he carried away as if they were great treasures. The sand dunes were dotted with shoes and burst balls and other things he had found.

The dogcatchers did not forget the dog from the sea. Every now and then they would return and try to catch him. They never could. The dog was too good at hiding and the sand dunes were too huge. The little sandy paths wound through them like paths in a maze.

The dog from the sea knew them all. Every tangled path in the grass. Every tunnel beneath the bushes. Every secret sandy hollow. Every lookout place.

One of the lookout places was right above the little white cottage. The dog from the sea depended on the cottage. Roasted chickens lived in the kitchen there, and whole boxes of dog biscuits lay unguarded on the grass.

There was a trash can like a treasure chest too. Sometimes it vanished at night, but sometimes it didn't. It depended on who was staying in the cottage.

On Saturday night, right before Lulu's father went to bed, he stepped outside and breathed a deep breath. There was a lovely

 33

smell of sea air and short green grass. There was an unlovely smell of something else.

"I'm *not!*" said Lulu's father. "I'm *just* not! I'm just not taking that *trash can* into the house at night!"

Chapter Three

Sunday

When Lulu and Mellie woke up on Sunday morning, there, right outside the window, was Lulu's father. He had a trash bag and a pointy stick and Lulu's seaside shovel for scooping. There was garbage all over the garden—not just the little bit of garbage that Lulu's family had thrown away, but also everything left behind from the people who had stayed in the cottage the week before.

"The dog from the sea must have come to visit!" said Lulu, and she was pleased.

"He made an awful mess," said Mellie.

"Perhaps we will have to take the trash into the house at night after all," said Lulu's mother at breakfast time, but she wrinkled her nose as she spoke.

"Absolutely not!" said Lulu's father. "I've thought of what to do. I'll get some big

rocks from the beach and use them as
weights on the lid of the can."

"You're not supposed to do that!" said
Lulu. "There's a sign on the beach that says
No stones or rocks to be taken away."

"I won't take them away," said Lulu's father.
"I'll just borrow them for a little while."

"Will you put them back?" asked Mellie.

"Of course."

"Carry them right across the sand dunes
back to the beach?"

"Absolutely."

"And put them exactly where you found
them? How will you remember?"

"I'll draw a map."

"What if someone sees you?" said Lulu.
"Even if you draw a map and even if
you take them back and even if they're
only borrowed, you'll still look like a
rock burglar!"

For a moment Lulu's father looked rather sad. He didn't want to look like a rock burglar. Then he had a good idea.

"I'll smuggle them! Under my shirt or hidden in a bag! I'll locate the rocks, draw a map, mark their positions, borrow them— *borrow,* not take!—and then I'll smuggle them across the sand dunes! And use them on the trash can lid!"

Lulu's father looked very happy at this thought. He was pleased to have an excuse to do some smuggling on his seaside vacation.

"It will be good for my fitness training," he said. "I've decided to run the next marathon! This vacation I am going to do push-ups and weights and a lot of running. Anyone who likes can come with me!"

"This vacation I am going to read and read," said Lulu's mother. "I never get time to read at home. I've brought six books, one for each day, and *War and Peace* for a spare! Anyone who likes can borrow the ones I'm not reading!"

"This vacation I'm going to make my kite *perfectly*," said Mellie. "Every part perfect, like the picture on the box. Anyone who likes can help me!"

"This vacation," said Lulu, "I'm going to find the dog from the sea, make friends with him, tame him so that he doesn't run away, and—"

That was as much as Lulu managed to say before everyone started talking at once, saying what a bad idea they thought it was, and how it could never happen, and even if it did, what then? It wouldn't be kind to the dog from the sea to make friends with him and tame him. He would have to be left behind at the end of the week anyway.

 39

"Why?" asked Lulu. "What about the more the merrier, as long as I clean up after them?"

"That's hamsters and goldfish and rabbits and things!" her mother told her. "Not dogs! Think of Sam!"

"Sam would hate it," said Lulu's father. "He's an only-dog sort of dog."

That was true.

Sam could put up with parrots and he really liked goldfish. He didn't mind guinea pigs. He was only slightly annoyed by hamsters and rabbits.

But dogs he could not stand!

Sam thought dogs were smelly and noisy and greedy. They were his least favorite animals, even worse than cats.

Sam didn't know, and would never have guessed, that he was a dog himself.

"But who will look after the dog from the sea?" asked Lulu.

"Someone," said her mother.

"Not us," said her father, and then both of them said, "Not sensible! Not going to happen! Not even slightly possible!"

Lulu did not argue. She had found that arguing only made people argue back. It was better, she thought, to do exactly as you liked, quietly, with no fuss. Besides, what did her crazy family know about possible and impossible?

As if it were even slightly possible that her father would ever run a marathon!

Or that her mother would read six books in six days ending with *War and Peace* (which she had been trying to read ever since before Lulu was born).

Or even that Mellie would perfectly finish her kite, which was already spread all over the living room floor with the string in knots and the instructions missing.

"Never mind," said Mellie. "I never bother with boring instructions anyway."

"How can you make it without instructions?" wondered Lulu.

"I'll just copy the picture on the box."

"It'll take ages."

"Not if you help," said Mellie, looking around to make sure Lulu's parents were out of the way, and adding, "You help me

42

with my kite and I'll help you with the dog from the sea."

Lulu thought about how much she liked Mellie, who never thought anything was impossible.

"I'll help you as soon as we come back from the beach," she promised.

The way to the beach was straight out the door and over the sand dunes.

A path of
soft, sliding
sand climbed
up and down.

A leg-aching sort of path.

"We should have brought camels," said
Lulu's father as they slipped and dropped
things and tumbled over Sam, who kept
stopping for rests
where people were
about to walk.

Lulu was looking out for the
dog from the sea. She had filled her
pockets with dog biscuits before she left
the cottage. Now she lagged behind the
others and scattered them along the path
as she walked.

Just in case, thought Lulu.

Not many people came to their end of the beach. Most of the other families on vacation were far away. The umbrellas and picnic blankets where they had set up their camps looked like tiny bright patches in the distance.

Lulu's family made a camp too, a very large one, because there seemed to be so many things they could not do without.

Books and shovels and training weights, the frisbee and the towels. The picnic blanket and picnic things. The windscreen because Sam did not like chilly breezes. Sam's beanbag, so that he could snooze in comfort, and, of course, his dog food dish and his water bowl and a big bottle of water.

The dog from the sea found his trail of biscuits very quickly, and after that it did not take him long to find Lulu and the camp. From high up on the sand dunes he watched everything that happened.
The longer he watched, the more interested he became.

   Some of the things he saw were very puzzling. Lulu's mother, for instance, reading her book, turning the pages, not looking up, saying, "Hmmm, hmmm," when anyone spoke to her. *A strange way to behave*, thought the dog from the sea.

Lulu and Mellie were not so mysterious. They were chasing a round toy that flew through the air. As soon as they caught it they flung it away. They made happy noises unless they fell over. Then they squealed. If they squealed very loudly the person with the book said, "Hmmm?"

But she still didn't look up.

Lulu's father was not mysterious at all. He was collecting things, just like the dog did himself sometimes. Safe at a distance, the dog watched him toil through the sand dunes—backward and forward, smuggling rocks.

Then there was Sam.

The dog from the sea had been so busy looking at the people that he did not notice Sam until Lulu's mother put down her book and called, "What about our picnic?"

Then he noticed him.

Sam ate biscuits and pizza and jam drops and wheat bread and sandwiches, and the dog from the sea watched every bite. He wanted the sandwiches so much he cried a little as he saw them vanish, but the thing he longed for most of all was Sam's water bowl.

The beach was a thirsty place for a dog to live. The golf course stream at one end was guarded by golfers. The kiddie pool at the other end was guarded by paddlers.

When the dog from the sea saw Sam's water bowl brimming with clear water he crept closer and closer.

The food was all gone. The last of the pizza and jam drops and wheat bread and sandwiches all eaten up.

Lulu's mother put down her book, stretched her arms, and wandered off to collect shells.

Lulu's father did some stretches and set off to jog along the surf.

Only Lulu and Mellie and Sam were left.

The dog from the sea was hardly frightened at all of people who were Lulu and Mellie's size. And he had a strong feeling that he could run faster than Sam.

And he was very thirsty. He took a step forward, and then another, creeping through the sand-dune grasses…then suddenly Sam saw him.

 49

"*RUFF! RUFF! RUFF!*" barked Sam.

"*RUFF! RUFF! RUFF!*" And he tumbled off his beanbag.

"*RUFF! RUFF! RUFF!*" And he actually set off at a teddy bear trot toward the dog from the sea.

The dog from the sea sank lower and lower into the blue-green grasses as Sam came near.

He sank until he was invisible.

Then he gave a great leap and jumped right over Sam.

He landed in front of the water bowl. There was a sound like a drain, and the bowl was empty—slurped dry in one enormous slurp by the dog from the sea.

"*RUFF!*" roared Sam.

The dog from the sea ran, trampling his great sandy paws over Sam's beanbag on the way.

"*RUFF!*" howled Sam furiously, and he would have gone after him if Lulu had not grabbed his collar.

"Shush!" she told Sam, while Mellie refilled his water bowl, and to the dog from the sea Lulu called, "Good dog! It's all right! Good dog!"

High on the sand dunes the dog heard and was happy.

He had never been called a good dog before.

He liked it.

Lulu and Millie did not see the dog from the sea again that day. In the afternoon they walked into the town to bounce on the giant trampolines. That was fun. Afterward they went back to the cottage to start work on Mellie's kite.

Even with all the family's help that was not easy at all.

Includes everything needed to build this magnificent kite! read the writing on the box.

Lulu's father said there had been a printing error. He said it should read *nothing* instead of *everything*.

The bare little cottage was not much help. It didn't contain any useful kite-making things. Just before the shops closed they sent Lulu's father out in the car to buy scissors and glue and something sharp that would drill tiny holes.

"And while you are shopping you might get a couple of new mugs," said Lulu's mother. "And some bread and some salad and some sausages and a can opener that works. And a dish towel or two would be useful…"

Lulu's father groaned. Shopping was his least favorite thing to do and driving through potholes was his second least favorite. He drove away before they could think of any more things they needed.

"Scotch tape," remembered Mellie, watching the dust fly up as he bumped down the road.

"More dog food and a frying pan,"

added Lulu's mother. "Oh well, we'll send him again tomorrow! Poor thing! Never mind. We'll be extra nice to him when he comes back."

They were very kind to Lulu's father when he came bumping home. They let him barbecue the sausages, and afterward they played softball with him and then they helped him pile his smuggled rocks onto the trash can lid, and then they all went to bed.

Everyone went to sleep at once.

Except Lulu.

Lulu thought about the dog from the sea.

She thought about the smuggled rocks piled up on the trash can.

And she thought how painful it would be if those rocks were to fall on anyone's nose.

As soon as Lulu had thought these thoughts she climbed out of bed.

And then out of the window.

Then she went to the trash can and began lifting the rocks from its lid. She had to concentrate hard while she was doing this, because of the danger of dropping them on her bare feet. She did not look up until she had lifted down the last rock, and then she nearly jumped out of her skin.

The dog from the sea was creeping toward her like a hungry wolf.

("I think I would have screamed," said Mellie, when Lulu told her the next day.)

Lulu managed not to scream. Instead she said, as she had said before, "Good dog! It's all right! Good dog!"

The dog's tail began to swing with pleasure.

"Good dog," said Lulu encouragingly, and she lifted the lid from the trash can and fished out a burned sausage.

The dog ate all the burned sausages, and he drank two buckets full of water (collected for him by Lulu by way of the bedroom window). Then he and Lulu sat down together, and Lulu petted him, being careful not to touch the itchy patches where his fleas had made him scratch away his fur. Often she said "Good dog" as she petted, and every time she said it the dog's tail beat with happiness.

That was how Lulu and the dog from the sea became friends.

Chapter Four

Monday and Tuesday

On Monday Lulu's family spent the day exploring the local fort. It had cannons around the walls and a telescope on top of the battlements. With the telescope you could look right over the sand dunes. Lulu looked for a long time while a fidgety line built up behind her, but she did not see the dog from the sea.

A chilly wind blew over the battlements, straight through their fleeces and cold on their skin.

"Let's go home and make my kite," said Mellie.

On the box of Mellie's kite, under, *Includes everything needed to build this magnificent kite!* it also said, *Not suitable for children under the age of 36 months.* Underneath this Lulu's father had written: *Or anyone living on a potholey road.*

The kite in the kit was plain white plastic. That was so that you could draw your own picture. This was the part that Mellie had looked forward to most. She planned to cover the white plastic with rainbow-colored seagulls.

It was a very big kite. It would take a lot of rainbow seagulls to cover the whole surface.

"Anyone who likes can draw seagulls on my kite," said Mellie, tipping out felt pens all over the floor.

The problem was, anyone couldn't.

The pens were all dried up. One
after another Mellie pulled off their lids,
discovered their ghostly shadows, and flung
them away.

"It's not fair!" she wailed.

Lulu did not think it was fair either.
"Brand new pens all dried up!" she
exclaimed indignantly.

"I didn't use them once!" said Mellie
sadly. "Well, once, maybe…Or a few times
…I'll never get this kite made. I might as
well stop trying."

Bump, bump, bump went the car through
the potholes on an emergency expedition
to save Mellie from despair. They bought
new pens and cotton candy and a mountain
of french fries with chili-cheese sauce. The
cotton candy got in their hair and the chili-
cheese sauce smelled much nicer than it

tasted, but by bedtime a flock of seagulls as bright as flowers blossomed across the kite.

And that was another day over.

The dog from the sea did not come creeping like a wolf that night. He came trotting down the garden path like a friend on a visit. He was very pleased indeed with his fries and chili-cheese sauce. He swallowed in big hungry gulps and drank a bucketful of water.

As he drank, Lulu noticed his paper-bag ears. They were all tangled up with bramble stems. The brambles were so knotted into his fur that Lulu could not pull them free.

"I'll have to get the kite scissors," she whispered to the dog. She was very surprised a moment later to hear a voice call, "Here!"

"Mellie!"

"I've been watching," said Mellie, passing

the scissors out of the window. "Be careful not to make him too tame, Lulu!"

"Why?" asked Lulu, beginning to snip.

"Oh," said Mellie slowly. "Because it might not be safe to be too tame…"

The bramble strands pulled loose. The dog shook his paper-bag ears back into their proper places.

"…if he doesn't want to be caught," said Mellie.

Until that moment the dog had not noticed Mellie.

Suddenly he did. Perhaps because the snipping had stopped. Maybe because his ears were free at last. Whatever the reason, the dog from the sea gave Mellie a swift glance. Sudden alarm seemed to show in his eyes. His body went still.

"Good dog! It's all right," Lulu told him. "Good dog!"

The alarm seemed to fade. Very slowly the dog's tail began swinging again.

"He trusts you," said Mellie.

He did, but he was still nervous. At the sudden rustle of the French fry bag he backed away. A moment later, when Lulu accidentally rattled the trash can lid, he vanished completely.

"He'll be back again tomorrow," said Lulu.

Tuesday was a day of gray skies and sudden showers.

"There's a cliff-top walk we really should try," said Lulu's father, getting out his map.

Sam knew about maps and very long walks and he went and hid behind the sofa.

"I know how he feels," said Lulu's mother, but she did not hide behind the sofa. She built a driftwood fire and settled down in front of it with her third vacation book.

Behind the sofa Sam found Mellie's kite box. A long smooth stick fell out when he pushed it. Sam chewed it to pieces.

The silvery driftwood burned with pale-blue flames, and the room became warm. Lulu and Mellie and Lulu's father bumped away in the car. Sam thought it might be safe to come out from behind the sofa. He settled down in front of the fire with a second long stick from the box...

"My kite struts!" shrieked Mellie the moment she walked through the door.

When she had calmed down a bit, Lulu's father explained that nothing in the world was easier to make than kite struts.

And that he would do it in a moment. Beautifully and perfectly. Better than the originals. Out of any old straight piece of washed-up driftwood they could find.

After that the whole family hunted for washed-up driftwood in straight enough pieces to make new struts for a kite. They hunted until it was too dark to see, but they didn't find any.

And then they went sadly back to the cottage and ate omelettes and chocolate cake to cheer themselves up. It was a rather dismal evening, despite the chocolate cake and the charm of the driftwood fire. Mellie put all her pieces of kite on the table, the seagull picture and the chewed wood and the tangled strings and the plastic loops for threading who-knew-what through (since the instructions had been lost) and she said to Lulu, "You said you'd help."

"I will help," said Lulu.

"Well, think of something!"

An idea came to Lulu like a present from the sky. She told her mother and her mother gave her a big happy hug. She told her father, and he said she was a genius. She would have told Mellie, but Mellie covered her ears and said, "Don't tell me, don't tell me, in case it doesn't work."

That night, the dog from the sea was waiting for Lulu. He ate omelette and toast and chocolate cake, a lot of dog food, and a large piece of cheese. More thorns and tangles were snipped from his fur. Once again, Mellie watched from the window, but this time he was much less nervous.

"I think he might like me after all," whispered Mellie.

"Of course he does," said Lulu.

 67

Chapter Five

Wednesday

They woke up on Wednesday to a day of bright sunshine.

"I am going shopping; I may be a while," said Lulu's mother, climbing into the car.

"What kind of shopping?" asked Mellie.

"Secret shopping," said Lulu's mother, and to Lulu she whispered, "Operation Kite!"

Then she bumped away down the dusty road with Sam to keep her company.

Lulu and Mellie and Lulu's father headed for the beach. It was a much easier journey over the sand dunes without Sam and his beanbag. Lulu's father went swimming, and Lulu and Mellie went to the kiddie pool. However, no one stayed in long because, as Lulu's father pointed out, the sea was very close to freezing and if it froze over completely they'd be stuck in the ice. Afterward, Lulu and Mellie went off to play, while Lulu's father did some exercises to get rid of the numbness in his hands and feet.

Lulu and Mellie had not been playing for more than five minutes when a head with paper-bag ears looked over the sand dunes.

The dog from the sea had come to play too.

At first he just played beside them. When Lulu and Mellie raced after the frisbee, the dog from the sea raced after an invisible

frisbee of his own.
When they
peered into
rock pools, he
peered into
rock pools close

by. When they paddled in the pools,
which were much warmer than the
sea, the dog paddled
too, sneezing at the
splashes. And then
they got out two
bottles of bubbles.
The dog
from the sea could
not resist the bubbles. He
raced to catch them,
snapped at them in
the air, and looked
astonished when they

vanished. He loved when Lulu and Mellie laughed at him. His tail wagged and his paper-bag ears flapped and he bounced like a dog on springs.

When Lulu's mother arrived with Sam and his beanbag and a thumbs-up sign for Lulu and a hug for Mellie and a picnic and a handful of dripping ice cream, the dog from the sea did not run away.

He stayed and shared the picnic.

He didn't come very close. He didn't quite trust Lulu's parents not to be secret dogcatchers, but still, he stayed.

If Sam had not been worn out by shopping he would not have let this happen. But shopping had tired Sam completely. He lay down on his beanbag and closed his eyes so that he could not see the dog from the sea, with the frisbee as a plate, eating hot dogs and sandwiches, and drinking water from Lulu's bucket.

"Now!" said Lulu's mother, when the picnic was all finished. "You'll never guess what I bought this morning, Mellie!"

"What?"

"A build-your-own-kite kit just like the one you had!" said Lulu's mother triumphantly. "So now we have all the pieces *and* new strings with no knots *and* the proper instructions!"

"Oh!" gasped Mellie, hugging her. "Was that what you thought of, Lulu, last night?"

"I told you I'd help!" said Lulu proudly, and her father said, "Come on! Back to the cottage, everyone, for Operation Kite!"

Operation Kite took Lulu's parents and Mellie all afternoon, and except for the seagull picture on the front, it was a brand-new kite.

 73

"It's the picture on the front that matters," said Mellie cheerfully.

Lulu did not help with the kite-making. Instead, she spent the afternoon on the grassy patch outside the house, playing with the dog from the sea.

It was very, very different from playing with Sam. If you threw a ball for Sam to fetch he would try not to look unless you happened to be someone he loved very much. If you were, he would get slowly to his feet. Slowly, slowly he would walk to the ball, pick it up in his teeth as if it tasted nasty, and then slowly bring it back to you, spit it out, and sigh.

The sigh meant, "Please don't do that again. I will not fetch it twice."

Very different from the dog from the sea, who hurtled after balls so fast he skidded and rolled in somersaults. Who could catch a frisbee in his teeth. Who understood the game of tag and played it around and around the little white cottage.

Lulu and the dog from the sea played so hard, they didn't notice the cottage owner coming silently along the path to the cottage.

The cottage owner liked to visit the cottage now and then, to check that her guests were behaving as she thought they should behave.

Just in case they weren't.

Lulu wasn't.

 75

Halfway along the path the cottage
owner saw Lulu and the dog from the sea.

She paused.
She got off her bike.
She glared.
She puffed with fury.
Then she turned
around and rode off again
as quickly as she could to call
the dogcatchers.

The dogcatchers came quickly with a cage,
a long stick with a collar on the end, and
a handful of dog biscuits, and the cottage
owner following behind.

It took Lulu a little while to understand what was happening. At first she just stood and stared, her hand on the neck of the dog from the sea. Then she saw the van and the collar on a stick and the cottage owner, very eager, rushing up with her bike.

Lulu screamed and clutched the dog from the sea.

"That's right, hang on to him!" screeched the cottage owner, while from inside the cottage ran Lulu's parents and Mellie, and Sam barking, "*RUFF! RUFF! RUFF!*"

"Stand still, *please!*" begged one of the two dogcatchers. "Oooooff!"

That was the sound made when Mellie flung herself headfirst into the nearest dogcatcher's stomach.

"*Mellie!*" exclaimed Lulu's mother, grabbing her.

 77

"*RUFF! RUFF! RUFF!*" roared Sam at the dogcatchers and the cottage owner and at the dog from the sea, trembling with fear under Lulu's hand.

"Get that dog!" shouted the wicked witch of a cottage owner. "He's a thief! He's a menace! He needs to be locked up!"

"*No!*" shouted Lulu, and she stopped holding on to the dog from the sea. She pushed him away and cried, "Run!"

There had been two friends playing, blue-green grass, and a blue and white sky.

Now there was noise and trouble and anger. And the dog from the sea was gone, running for his life.

That night Lulu waited and waited, but the dog from the sea did not come to visit the cottage.

 78

"Do you think he's thinking of me like I am thinking of him?" she asked Mellie.

"Yes," said Mellie.

Much later in the night Mellie said, "I think you should stop climbing in and out of the window."

"I can't get to sleep."

"No one could get to sleep," said

Mellie, "if they kept climbing in and out of a window."

"Why aren't you sad?" demanded Lulu.

"I am sad," said Mellie. "About the poor dog from the sea, I'm sad! About how frightened he was, and how he looked at you to see if it was true, and how he saw that it was true, and ran, I'm sad about that! I helped, didn't I? I charged that dogcatcher as hard as I could!"

"Yes, you did," admitted Lulu.

"But I am not completely sad because I can't help feeling happy about my kite. I thought we'd never fix it, and now we have, and it's perfect. Don't you think that's good?"

"You know I do," said Lulu. "It was me that thought of the way to fix it."

"Tomorrow," said Mellie, "we can fly my kite on the beach. It will show for miles and miles. The dog will see it and come running."

That was a happy thought.

Lulu fell asleep thinking it.

Chapter Six

Thursday and Friday

Early on Thursday morning Mellie woke everyone up, hurried them through breakfast, and chased them out of the house.

"What's all this pushing and rushing?" demanded Lulu's father. "It's the last day of the vacation! Shouldn't we make the most of it and have a little peace?"

"It's because it's the last day!" said Mellie.

"What do you want peace for, anyway?" asked Lulu.

"I still haven't flown my kite!" said Mellie.

Lulu's parents looked at each other.
Then out the window.

"Mellie…" began Lulu's mother, but
Mellie would not listen. Over the sand
dunes she raced the family and onto the
wide sunny beach.

Not a breath of wind was blowing.

Not a breath of wind blew all that day.

They tried the beach and they tried the park and they tried the high place on the cliffs where the fort stood. They discovered that no amount of running and tossing and adjusting and untangling will make a kite fly without any wind.

It was the last day of the vacation, and no kite flew. No dog from the sea saw it and came running. And nothing, not paddling, nor fair rides, nor even takeout food from the Golden Lotus could make Lulu and Mellie happy.

The grown-ups were sad too. They had worked hard to make that kite fly, spent a lot of money, and driven through a great many potholes. They were unhappy about the dog from the sea as well. Secretly, they took turns going to look for him. Lulu's father went for a long marathon-training run all through the sand dunes with dog

85

biscuits in his pockets. Lulu's mother walked in the opposite direction with a bucket and a bottle of water. She stopped to talk with the people from the hot dog and ice cream stall and with the lady at the bucket and shovel shop.

Nobody had seen the dog from the sea.

In the evening, promises were made to Mellie. "We have to get an early start in the morning," Lulu's mother told her. "I'm sorry, Mellie, but I have to be at work at the hospital by lunchtime…"

Mellie nodded. Lulu's mother was a nurse, and both Lulu and Mellie understood that nurses have to be at work when they are expected.

"But the first windy day at home that everyone is free we will all stop whatever

we're doing and rush to the park with your
kite! We promise! Don't we, Lulu?"

"Yes," said Lulu, "but…"

But it won't be the same, she nearly said.

"But what?" asked her mother.

"Nothing," said Lulu, because what
was the use of saying what everybody knew.

The bare little cottage was tidied and
cleaned. Bags were packed. Sand drifts
were swept from the corners of floors. Last
of all, Lulu and Mellie and Lulu's father
smuggled the trash can lid rocks back over
the sand dunes. With the help of the map
they put them back on the beach in their
old locations.

"They look like they've never been
moved!" said Lulu's father.

That night the trash can lid was left
unguarded. Now that the dog from the sea

87

had disappeared, he no longer seemed such
an impossible idea to Lulu's parents.

"I bet Sam would have gotten used to
him, after a while," they said, and they
understood when Lulu put the leftovers
from the Golden Lotus in a bowl beside
the trash can, just in case.

They understood, too, when Mellie could
not bear to pack her unflown kite. "Just let

me keep it like it is until morning! Just to look at," she begged.

"All right, Mellie."

They even understood when Lulu insisted on keeping the bedroom window wide, wide open.

"But no getting out and camping by the trash can!" said Lulu's father, astonishing Lulu, who had not even told Mellie of this very private idea. "Promise?"

"Promise," said Lulu reluctantly.

"Go to sleep quickly then," said Lulu's parents, who kissed them and went to bed.

Going to sleep quickly was not something that Lulu and Mellie usually managed. Usually they chatted for hours.

This time, however, they went to sleep quickly.

Mellie woke with a jump in a room full of gray light.

It was dawn and it was cold, and the air was full of a thin sound. At the window the curtains were streaming like flags into the room.

"Lulu! Lulu!" whispered Mellie. "The wind is blowing!"

The wind *was* blowing, and Lulu's watch said half past four in the morning. They had hours and hours before the grown-ups woke.

They did not pause for a moment.

Lulu put on her sandals.

Mellie picked up her kite.

First Lulu, then Mellie, climbed out of the window.

The food from the Golden Lotus was still untouched in the bowl by the trash.

"But he'll see the kite," said Lulu and followed Mellie across the patch of blue-green grass, into the sandy paths that wound through the sand dunes, and onto the empty beach.

A strong straight wind was blowing. A perfect flying wind. The kite, with its flock of bright seagulls, leaped into the sky.

From the moment the kite took off, Lulu and Mellie forgot everything but the need to hold on to it. It pulled on the strings like something alive. No flock of seagulls had ever soared higher.

The kite raced in front of the wind, and Lulu and Mellie raced along the beach behind it, each clinging to a kite handle.

"Hold tight with both hands!" screamed Mellie, and it lifted them as they ran, so that they hardly felt their feet touch the

 91

sand. They felt nothing but the huge tug
of the strings in their hands, and they saw
nothing but sky.

For a long time, an unmeasurable amount
of time, it was like running in an airy
dream.

Then Lulu tripped and fell.

The kite-string handle flew out of her
hand, and the kite, suddenly unbalanced,

spun in a spiral, poised in the air for a moment, and then dived its whole flock of rainbow seagulls headfirst into the sand dunes.

"Oh!" gasped Mellie, while Lulu picked herself up. "My kite, my kite!" She started running to where it had fallen.

Lulu followed more slowly, gathering the kite strings and feeling her bumped knees. She had time to look around and see where they were. They were on a strange part of the beach, with unknown sand dunes, far away from the little white cottage.

Mellie was nowhere in sight.

Nothing Lulu recognized was anywhere in sight.

Then, from somewhere high above, Mellie screamed.

Lulu began to run.

In those unknown sand dunes the gray-leaved, orange-berried bushes grew very close and thorny. The sandy paths were narrower, made for rabbits, not people. The hollows were deep and unexpected. The grasses grew over them and hid them, so they opened suddenly, like traps.

"Lulu!" cried Mellie, and Lulu called back, "Where are you? Where are you?" and stumbled as she hurried.

It took a long time to find Mellie.

It was like trying to find someone in a maze.

But at last, there she was. Tumbled into a hollow, clutching her kite, and trying not to cry.

"I'm all right," she told Lulu, with her eyes screwed tight shut. "But I hurt my foot! I hurt it really…" She gave a little sob. "I don't want to look. Is it bleeding?"

It was bleeding. Mellie had caught it on thorns, tripped, and fallen with it twisted beneath her. Already her ankle was puffy and swollen.

"Don't touch it!" she begged when Lulu bent to look, and then she did a very strange thing.

She yawned.

The earliness of the morning, the fright and the pain, were suddenly too much for Mellie. She switched them off.

She put her head on Lulu's lap and went to sleep.

For a long time Lulu sat thinking. She did not know what to do. She couldn't leave Mellie and go for help. It would take ages, and besides, she was not at all sure, even with the kite strings to follow, that she would ever find Mellie again. And it was perfectly obvious that Mellie could not walk back on such a bad foot.

Nor could Lulu carry her.

We could shout for help, Lulu thought. She tried a small shout. "Help! Help!"

The wind blew the words away and lost them in the grasses.

I've got to think! she told herself fiercely and closed her eyes to help herself think better.

A great brightness woke them both.

Blue and pink and gold. The morning sky shone above their faces, edged with the dark shadows on the long sand-dune grasses.

And high above, on the edge of the hollow, they saw something else.

A long-legged, scruffy, wind-blown outline of a dog.

A dog who, from far away, had seen a kite and come running.

The dog from the sea looked down at Lulu and Mellie, dark against the bright sky, like an illustration from a fairy tale.

The dog from the sea stared at Lulu and Mellie in great surprise. He had not expected to find them when he had come running to investigate the kite. What were they doing so far from their home? Where were their grown-ups, and what about Sam?

The dog from the sea tilted his head with its paper-bag ears one way and then the other, trying to understand.

They were talking. Hurriedly and worriedly.

"Go with him! Maybe he'll take you back to the cottage!"

"What, and leave you here?"

"You could."

"You know I wouldn't!"

"I'm all right, Lulu, really I am. It hardly hurts if I keep still."

"What if you try and stand?"

"I don't know. Maybe, if I had a bandage for my foot. In case it bleeds again."

A ribbon of kite tail made a sort of bandage, and then Lulu said, "Just try. I'll help. I'll balance you…"

"Ouch! *Ouch!* It's too tight! Don't pull! Let me go!"

Mellie fell back down into the sand, peeled off the kite tail, and whimpered a little because her foot was now very painful. The whimpering worried the dog. He backed away, whining.

"Good dog. It's all right," called Lulu soothingly as she hugged poor Mellie, but she did not sound all right.

Neither did Mellie.

"What'll we do?" asked Mellie between very damp hiccups. "How'll anyone ever know we are here?"

 100

"They'll come and look for us," said Lulu bravely. "As soon as they get up and see we're not there…"

"How'll they know which way to look?"

"I don't know," admitted Lulu. "Maybe they'll find our footprints…"

Lulu paused.

"They never will," said Mellie and sobbed, a real sob, and then another and another.

"Oh, don't cry!" Lulu begged so miserably that the dog from the sea tumbled into the hollow to comfort them both. He licked salty fingers and rubbed his ragged head into their hands, not knowing what to do.

And then all at once, he knew exactly what to do.

Like a picture in his head the dog from the sea saw the white cottage and the grown-ups belonging to his two unhappy friends.

They would have to be fetched.

He left Lulu and Mellie as suddenly as he had found them, leaping out of the hollow and vanishing among the sand dunes. He did not want to fetch the grown-ups. He did not want to go back to where the dogcatchers had been. For all he knew they might be there still.

But he could not think of anything else to do.

So he did it.

His long legs raced across the beach as fast as the cloud shadows raced across the sea. Mellie's kite-tail bandage, picked up at the last moment as he left, streamed behind him like a banner. In minutes he was back at the cottage, and there were the grown-ups, calling and searching up and down the sand dunes and in and out the house.

Sam saw him first.

"*RUFF!*" barked Sam but not very fiercely. He was too tired to be fierce. He had been up for ages with no breakfast, trudging through the sandy paths, trying to find the girls.

"*RUFF!*" barked Sam, but he didn't really mean it.

"WOOFF! WOOFF! WOOFF!" replied the dog from the sea.

"Listen!" called the grown-ups, and they both came running.

"Look! Look! It's the dog from the sea!"

"Oh!" cried Lulu's mother, and she picked up the kite ribbon.

"He knows where they are!" Lulu's father exclaimed.

"WOOFF!" commanded the dog from the sea.

Anyone could tell what he wanted.

So Mellie and Lulu were rescued.

First came the dog from the sea.

Next came Lulu's father (who was very glad he had done so much training for when he might run a marathon).

Then Lulu's mother, keeping up very well considering she had spent the whole

week reading book after book (although not
War and Peace).

Last of all, Sam.

Sam did not run to the rescue; he
walked.

Sam was only a little way along the journey
when they all came back. He stopped when
he saw the dog from the sea.

The dog from the sea stopped when he
saw Sam.

But Lulu's father (who was carrying
Mellie) said, "Don't be silly, you two!"

And Lulu's mother (who was carrying the kite) said, "You might as well make friends!"

And Lulu put them each on a kite-tail leash and led them back to the cottage, where Mellie's sprained foot was bathed and bandaged with an ice pack.

"There's no time for telling you off!" said Lulu's parents, as the bandaging took place. "But if there was…"

Luckily there wasn't. There was only time to fling the last things in the car and somehow find an extra place on the backseat for Sam, because…

"You're never going to leave with that dog!" demanded the cottage owner, arriving just in time to see the dog from the sea being coaxed into the car.

"We are," said Mellie, smiling up at her. "Aren't you happy?"

"Happy! What are you thinking? Isn't one dog enough?"

"The more the merrier," said Lulu's mother.

"He's been wonderful," said Lulu's father.

"Well, good riddance, I say," said the cottage owner, glaring. "But don't say I didn't warn you! He's trouble, that dog! He's a thief! He's a menace!"

"He's a hero," said Lulu, and she gave the dog from the sea one last hug before she climbed into her seat beside Mellie and

Sam. "He's ours and we love him, and we're taking him with us!"

Bump! went the car, through the first of the potholes, and then they were on the way home.